MW00989233

THE ACTIVIST

THE ACTIVIST

RENEE GLADMAN

KRUPSKAYA · 2003

ACKNOWLEDGMENTS

An earlier version of *The Interrogation* was published in *Conjunctions 35*. Grateful acknowledgment to Bradford Morrow and Mei-mei Berssenbrugge.

My deepest thanks to Rachel Bernstein for her enormous love, to Thalia Field for talking me through this, to Aja Duncan for her constancy, and to my sisters, Gwen and Vanessa, and my Mama, Harriette, for their humor and support.

This final version of *The Activist* is indebted to the eyes of Rachel Bernstein, Melissa Buzzeo, Aja Duncan, Thalia Field, Rachel Levitsky, Alice Notley, and Martin Riker.

The phrase "A slow over-hunting," which appears in *White City II,* is quoted from "Autobiography" by Thalia Field.

Any resemblance found to actual persons, events, emotions, or gestures is merely an imaginary figment of the persons, events, emotions, and gestures found henceforth.

Copyright © 2003 Renee Gladman
Cover Design: Frank Mueller
Cover Image: Matthew Nichols

Distributed by Small Press Distribution, Berkeley
800-869-7553
spdbooks.org

ISBN 1-928650-18-X

KRUPSKAYA
PO Box 420249
San Francisco, CA
94142-0249
krupskayabooks.com

CONTENTS

for Stefani Barber
graced this

TOUR

There,

those buildings made entirely of glass, busses
streaming between

mean the city is integrated.

But over here,

where the sun sinks behind the mountains,

these our jails, our isolated

have seized the periphery.

This our downtown.

I dream them here, the activists, who are recurring. I walk down this street convinced that I
am on the cusp of something. Many things oc-
cur, but all at a tremendously slow pace. Then—
and this happens every time—trucks come reel-
ing around the corner, trying to flatten me. I
know it's the radicals because they are always
leaning out the windows, shouting slogans. The
dream ends as I dive behind a trash bin, the same
bin every time.

It is dark here without the sun; I'm waiting for the street lamps to come on. I don't think I'll move until they do.

Standing here, doing nothing, I realize the problem with the activists. They are covert, and when you are covert, you miss out on the best of the information.

Everything one needs to know is right out in the open.

The street, illuminated.

I am studying the interiority of criminals—once they are captured or become fugitive, the way their emotions manifest. If you can be a person only when you are violating city power, what happens when you must restrain yourself from such violations, when you are in hiding?

This is our café. Reporters' lounge.

Over there,

between the black couple and those students, that fresh little girl.

This is a new era of reporting, where every idea lights upon the public with the vivacity of a pre-pubescent.

The street curves. And when I'm here, the thick certainty of this: we are surrounded on all sides.

The activists watch us. They record our gestures so that later they can emulate them. They go to our work and insist they are us . . . do us better than we ever could . . .

Whenever I say that I begin to sweat.

These walls, peeling and skanked up. But underneath, this story:

Years ago I followed a group whose prime objective was to enfeeble the government's domestic identification system. That's right—the Department of Social Security. They wanted to alter the names of every white man above the age of twenty to Jonah Smith, then Jonah Smith, junior, then Jonah Smith, the third, infinitesimally—

Do you know Smith? He was the guy leading the crackdown against illegal immigration. They got caught and blamed their indictment on me—the sympathetic field reporter. It was a scene.

On these walls they exacted revenge against me. Now, I'm protected.

Our factories.

And this unbearable smell. We don't know if it's bread baking or some kind of toxic fume. But I bring everybody here.

I do these things, these tours, because of that dilapidated area there. This whole quadrant before me.

Because it is in ruins.

Because there is nothing this way.

And I anticipate what the activists will bring me from whichever worlds they choose for escape.

From these pockets in which I wait, report, wait.

TOP OF THE HOUR

Officials pursue activists over rocky terrain in search of answers. "We want to make sure anger does not ruin these kids," Daniel Sharpe of the Brendan Seize Unit (BSU) confides, "but it's like pushing against water."

Investigators combed shards from the collapsed bridge for signs that it had been blown apart. "I have a feeling that Monique Wally and her group are behind this. What we have is a smell of iron burning, but no visual evidence on site." Sharpe and his BSU team have joined with local police and the FBI to solve the encrypted crime.

"Only the time of day distinguishes these so-called dissidents from terrorists. Had they blown that bridge an hour earlier or an hour later, we would have had a lot of death on our hands."

The bridge remains intact today, despite reports that it is long gone. A team of specialists from the Institute of Explosive Applications in Toronto, Ontario, is expected to settle the matter by mid-week. "These scientists are the elite among their field. We have every faith that they will acknowledge the violence done to the bridge," the President assured viewers today.

"This kind of presence makes my people nervous," Sharpe declares to an audience of reporters at a noon press conference. "In a time where we have to face some real live threats, we mustn't get derailed by phantoms." Following this admission, a reporter from the *Daily* challenged Sharpe on his organization's interpretation of the term "presence," to which Sharpe declined to respond.

"I allowed myself to be punctured by stones during the pursuit. It felt like the manly thing to do. I mean, these are the kind of people that need to be rounded up and quickly prosecuted . . . this pain I endured for my country," added one of Sharpe's men.

Though Canadian scientists say the bridge is intact, Daniel Sharpe remains convinced that it has been blown apart. "I need someone with keen eyes," he told the *Daily*. The President says that Sharpe is his "best man" and he is determined to stand by him in light of the new information.

Today the first commuters attempted to cross the bridge despite a heavy police presence. Harvey Pratt, a 45-year-old attorney, spoke from his car, "They are blaring signs demanding that we stop. But what do they want us to do? We've all got kids to feed. Personally, I'm tired of pretending that I don't see the bridge."

A possible conspiracy, or just old-fashioned con-fusion, caused leaders to retract earlier statements about the bombing of J. Gifford Bridge. A spokesperson for Senator Glee reported, "Now that the Senator has seen documents nearly prov-ing some type of fire in or on the bridge, he is prepared to allocate funds necessary for bring-ing the guilty to justice."

A forty-eight-page report, released today by Canadian officials, suggests that there never was a bridge. "Not clear it was a crossing point," the document reads. With the announcement, the President ordered troops to return to the site to oversee further investigations.

"I am committed to bringing these manipulators to justice. I swear on my heart that Americans will not be rabble-roused." The final words of the President's weekly radio report.

"This is truly embarrassing for the administration," a specialist on perception theory and war, who asked to remain anonymous, confided. "What we have is an extreme form of civil disobedience. Something our public has never seen before. This is the situation we're facing: a shockingly high number of witnesses claim that the bridge is in perfect form, the President of our nation is convinced that the bridge has been exploded, another group asserts that the bridge has collapsed, not exploded, and a handful of researchers contests that there ever was a bridge. Now imagine how this sounds to people in other countries, or just on the other coast."

THE iNTERROGATiON

Farther along, members of the CPL wait in front of a popular café—

Still there because they love me,

he thinks.

This walking,

he'll say when he arrives,

was difficult for me. There were obstacles in the street—though I can't prove it—every time I hit one falling on my head was the result, and by the time I recovered from the fall there was no accessible memory.

Seeing them in their glorious postures Lomarlo wants to yell encouragement, but he's too tired to say the words—

These are good friends, though. They know how to wait. Soon I'll arrive and we'll eat.

Then he trips and falls into a pothole. When twenty minutes later he reaches them, they are having an argument about eggs.

Monique is saying:

We have to think seriously here . . . the signals are always . . . scrambled . . . we've got to break the barrier . . . fuck their system from the inside . . . no this ain't the pacifist movement . . . we've outlived that occasion . . .

While Stefani shouts:

Yeah let's lay 'em all out,

during M.'s ellipses.

Lomarlo considers:

This might not be about eggs and perhaps I'm not supposed to hear. But these are my comrades! They're smiling at me. One has his hand on my shoulder, expecting me to ease into this conversation when I have been struggling to get here, when the worst things have happened to me.

Freddie embraces the newcomer:

So Lomo, what do you think?

I just want to eat. I never care what it is.

Apparently his friends agree, as each has walked away, presumably to secure a table.

This is the warmest day we've had so far . . . yes it really is,

he repeats to himself, trying to keep his mind off his hunger. When the others return they stand around him, smoking. Monique steps away from the group, shuffling papers:

Listen up, crew. I have made some diagrams of the inner labyrinth. These marks in blue indicate our points of entry—

Don't be so—

Lomarlo snaps, delirious with hunger:

So . . . you know . . .

The group finds a table. Freddie studies the sky then each of their faces:

It's beautiful today. Are we sure?

I'm sure,

Lomarlo affirms.

Breakfast is going well, though since L.'s out-
burst, they've been sitting in silence. Alonso
decides to ask a question:

Lomo, what happened to you last night?

This sudden interest inspires the newcomer to
self-reflection. He gazes inward:

*They want my story. When I was young this is what
I imagined—a group turning to me, members with
a cock to their heads, awaiting me. Not like the
time I nearly fell into the fire while Freddie was
searching for wood and something in that search
kept him away for hours as I lay there. And our
other friends, now long gone, wandering in their
drugs—*

Lomarlo shakes his head,

These are not my memories.

He shakes his head again, more violently,

Where are my memories?

Then he locks onto a series of aerials flying an elaborate pattern.

Birds don't fly that low,

he observes with growing paranoia.

A mosquito buzzes by. He moans,

What's that?

Turning down a path, away from the birds,

Got to get away but quietly so the flies don't notice me.

He crouches behind a trash bin, waits—

Stefani zips his sweatshirt shut and pushes him out the door. No more memory. Outside the café, he looks around himself. The light is low, as after a storm or shortly before sunset, or as a result of wearing shades, or some doom is coming. He feels his hand flapping against his skin but does not know what he's looking for.

Stefani, what's on me?

Can't say without looking at you.

Well, look at me!

But you said not to!

Where did everybody go?

Ikea.

Why?

To blow it up.

What are you doing?

Keeping my eye on you.

How, if you don't look at me?

I've been listening for you.

Where have we been all day?

There, eating eggs.

To himself:

I can't believe I've been away from myself for so many hours, and I don't feel the least bit rested. In fact, what's all this on my shoulders? What's pouring out of my eyes and toes? Not my chi. Where's that?

Stefani holds his hand, leading the way to their next meeting. He uses the downtime to put order to his mind.

Now let's see . . . where is that chi?

Once again inside his mind, walking quickly through rooms with his head down. He glimpses a photo on the floor. It's damaged, ripped into several pieces. Nevertheless he recognizes the face. His. Taken some years ago.

41

I remember that store I'm posed in front of. I used to meet the group there. How did this picture get separated from the other snapshots that were taken? And why is it destroyed?

He looks around with alarm, as if caught in something. Then snaps,

This is my mind, only I have the right to be here,

against a creeping sense of being post-invasion.

The next morning Lomarlo wakes with his ass pressed against Alonso's hip. He's recalling his dreams, monotonous as always but with a new array of characters who're much more violent than those of the nights before. —Wait. He thinks it's Alonso. The pain in his ass is the same, so it must be. Yet other than what he knows to have existed in the past, there is no further evidence. Soon he'll have to turn around to see. But there is no light, no sun shining through his blackened windows. Plus, if he turns around and it's not Alonso, he'll want to squash whoever it is, unless that person's stronger. No, the best way to find out is to get the person to speak. He begins:

In one of my dreams people were playing with fire-arms and I was not sure what to do.

Silence.

He adds:

There was glass everywhere. I wonder if I screamed. Did I scream?

Silence, as that following cell death. He imagines himself embraced by a lifeless form, and with a mixture of disgust and anticipation, reaches back to tap the offending bone. It jumps.

Waking again, late afternoon, Lomarlo looks around himself and supposes he's slept for a week. This time he is not in bed but at a table, with the group, in front of a plate of eggs. He's trying to get his wits about him, but something's wrong,

What the hell is she saying?

Lomarlo consults interiorly:

*That is not regular language. It's a code and every-
body knows it but me. Monique keeps saying, Ha
chini chini, and the rest of them nod their heads.
It's because I fell asleep . . . they're punishing me,
knowing I would forget this training. No, not the
CPL. Maybe the SFF, but never the CPL. I've just
got to relax . . . flow into this.*

He leans back in his chair, clears his mind, then
releases:

Ma chanic daravici delimatu,

slowly, without committing to any particular
inflection.

The group's response is unsurprising —faces turn
to him. He realizes:

*Damn, I should've asked a question. They would
have been forced to answer.*

Monique continues her monologue. She says many things, but *ha chini chini* is the most recurring.

I keep thinking about those words . . . I know them . . .

Stefani pokes him in the side with her elbow and whispers:

Isa uma kuni. Monique ma uma kuni.

He shakes her off.

Argh! What's this? Something's sticking me.

He reaches under his ass and finds some pieces of wire. He exclaims:

Ja se pa cahini.

Then clamps his hand over his mouth.

Freddie grabs the wire from him and places it in a box. The box claims Lomarlo.

The last time I was in a box it was spring,

he recalls,

The old group had gone downtown to sell papers, while I stayed behind to clean up. We were renting a small room in the old warehouse district. Somebody left a box open, the larger kind used when mailing banners overseas, and I stepped back into it. Lay there for hours, not because I couldn't get up but because I was comfortable there. I couldn't remember against whom we were fighting. Lying there I thought, On my back and safe in this tiny room, I want to think about my enemies. It was easy. No one intruded, everything was fine. I concentrated. However, the image never surfaced. That's not true. Several images came to me, but none of them seemed right. I was looking for something truly sinister. I kept saying, This couldn't be the enemy, discarding the idea.

Members of the CPL group, apprehended today by armed forces, have refused to answer investigators' questions regarding the bombing of
the J. Gifford Bridge. The leader of this extrem-
ist group, known primarily for its attacks on
"corporate disintegrity," denies any interest in
activism. "First of all," Monique Wally says, "it
is impossible to live in this country and think of
oneself as a group." David Sharpe, chief investi-
gator of the Brendan Seize Unit (BSU), revealed

to reporters that the leader would not admit to
"living a life among people." "If we can't even
get across the idea of people . . ." he complained.
"Instead of a hunger strike . . . it's as though
they are issuing a logic one"—but then immediately added that he didn't know what he meant
by that. Confession at this juncture seems un-
likely.

THE BRiDGE

A group of suburbanites, identifying themselves as "J. Gifford Commuters," have shut down Gifford Street to protest the bridge situation. Among the swarm of impassioned demonstrators, several key ideas circulated. Most seriously, the demand for "prioritized normalcy."

"I am not entirely sure these people are who they say they are. How can they be serious? I mean, look here [pointing to the bridge]. This is the barest remains of a bridge. Smell the air. What else is there to say?" Mr. Sharpe said, speaking to reporters this afternoon.

"You can't keep us back," a woman yelled from the audience when Sharpe paused to take a breath. "Nothing is worth this inconvenience," the man behind her added. And before Sharpe could continue, a near-violent chant of "reopen the bridge" erupted from the gathering.

The most outspoken of the demonstrators was a woman who gave only "Shirley" when asked her name. In fact, the rally proved plentiful of middle-aged adults unwilling to disclose their identities to the public. As of press time, *Daily* staff managed to collect one complete name: Alonso Mendoza. However, Mr. Mendoza was not present at this afternoon's event. The specifics of his relationship to those in attendance are unclear, but his name was the one thing that at least seventy percent of the group mentioned. Officials are baffled by the Commuters' demands.

Efforts to locate Alonso Mendoza, reported ring-leader of the Commuters, have been unsuccess-ful thus far. "All we have is this: he's a bit younger than the rest," said Daniel Sharpe, "and we're going with the assumption that Mendoza is an alias."

"Mendoza . . . Mendoza," a protestor, who stepped aside to answer questions, contemplated, "Yes, that name does sound familiar. But . . . I don't think I know him." Authorities insist the key to resolving the conflict lies within that thirty percent of the Commuters who are emotionally bound to the group but lack the rank to know the identity of their leader. "They are the ones who are most likely to leak something huge, and when they do we'll be there to lap it up," boasted one of Sharpe's lieutenants.

Three men—Al Mendoza, Alejandro Mendoza, and Alpine Mencini—were questioned at police headquarters about their political affiliations. An anonymous source admitted to the possibility that investigators were "grasping and falling on straw." But he reiterated that citizens must maintain their loyalty and commitment to the administration.

A crisp and sunny fall morning amplifies a concerted effort. It is the fifth straight day of protests, and the question of demonstrations carrying over to the weekend remains uncertain. "We've got to get these people out of here," Sharpe said. And in a moment of frustration, he blurted out: "Look [running toward the bridge], this creek is full of rubble, this emptiness here . . . it's where there used to be a bridge. If you try to cross, you will crash and harm yourself—most likely, die. Please go home and feed your pets and children."

"I am surprised to see our government behave this way," "Terry," a Commuter, exclaimed. "We know this is some kind of federal cover-up, and we won't leave until we get to the truth." Specialists from Canada's Institute of Explosive Applications, who assisted during the initial investigation of the J. Gifford dilemma, have been recalled by the President. "We are bringing these researchers back because their third opinion [that there never was a bridge] puts our current opposition in a vague light. We want to give them another chance to see this thing that is so testifiably in ruins before us," Mr. President declared yesterday in front of barricades sequestering the contentious site.

This morning, forces stormed the homes of Altar Mendlesohn, Alvin Mendocci, Alsana Mendoza, and Alonso Mitchell in search of the spurious leader of the Commuters, now accused of three felony counts of conspiratorial behavior. When asked the status of the "separate" criminal investigation of the CPL, the organization most likely behind the bridge's destruction, Daniel Sharpe of the BSU refused to speak. This statement was released to the press earlier today: "Americans need to understand that silence is sometimes necessary when one is engaged in a psychological war. And that is exactly what we are fighting here. There are too many people using our honesty with the American people for their own selfish gain. Our top priority is to disable the coagulation of all so-called angry people, be they commuters, activists, what have you."

THE STATE

Whether this is a dream in which I'm captured or I've been captured and made to think I'm in a dream, I can't figure. In one moment, the scenery is indistinguishable from that to which I'm accustomed: I sit at this table, I lay my hands on its surface. But in the next moment, I can't feel my hands and this table pushes against me. I detect the presence of others.

But why confuse me? I'm innocent. I have done nothing but wake and sleep. I have not left the house; I have not made any phone calls. I'm in the same clothes and, except when dreaming, in the same mood. To the first person who asks, I willingly disclose my full name, my place of birth, my age, and my sun sign. I have nothing to hide. All I have done is sit at this table awaiting the group, whom I have not seen in days.

To be clear, I'm not against the possibility that I'm dreaming. In a way, that reality would be what I always wanted. I have never been a good dreamer, so if it's true . . . if this were a dream, I could say I have transcended my usual monotony. I would have proof of my subconscious. However, there is some clue in the body. If I had been sitting at my table and, after hours of contemplation, had fallen asleep and into this imaginary world, then my body should, in a crucial sense, be out of time. So why is my hair growing? And why do I think about hunger? Whoever has captured me and is playing this inhuman trick is not the smartest of criminals. If you want a person to believe that he is dreaming, when in fact he is locked to a chair on drugs, you have to remove his body from time. You have to feed him to keep his mind off his body. Or do you? I can't figure out which is the right indicator of being in time: feeling hungry or satiated. But I do know there is a discrepancy.

—I think I said that last part out loud because something has swung and bounced off my face, and now I am on the floor. I am on my back, looking at the ceiling, which is covered in wires and mirrors and loaves of bread. Legs of pants with militaric creases surround me; congealed body water falls on my cheeks and slides into my ears. I hear an electronic drone, a wall of noise, then luminousless silence.

—A moment later, I'm feeling particularly at home, but I remember what has just happened to me. I look at my hands, trying to place the last encounter in a circuit of time, and wish to fan myself to lessen the impact of my ineptitude. When I turn my head and see someone familiar at the other end of the table, I lose confidence that this is my dining room. Though we are close enough that we could extend our arms and almost touch, he appears unaware of me. In fact, there is someone sitting in front of him. I watch the former move his mouth while the latter scribbles frantically across a page. The synchronicity of their action reminds me of factory machines. What, in itself, is so innocent— speech or penmanship—reeks of evil in this room. I don't think my friend knows where he is. His mouth moves incessantly, but his manner is not his own. What did they do to him? Seeing him violated in this way infuriates me. Soon I will have to smash my fist through the table—that is, if my arms are free. But I bet this is what they want. I'll beat my fists against the unyielding wood and, by that act of defiance, incriminate myself. What good is evidence, though, when it is gathered in a non-existent place?

* * *

I have not said anything for some time because
I have been struggling against subjugation: I'm
in a dank room, surrounded by more pleats. The
drugs they forced on me have seized power over
my nervous and muscular systems, making me
want to talk and reveal my true emotions. I have
been invaded and almost occupied to the core.
As the chemical levels uninhibiting me increase,
I can no longer postpone the moment. I begin,
with uncharacteristic honesty:

*A day last fall, I set out to take a walk across a
bridge. Fallen leaves, brown and gold, ran along
its sides. I studied the leaves because I thought there
was something representative in them. I am always
looking for analogies, thinking that eventually I'll
stumble upon a relation that will give a face to this
world, that will stand in for these vague impres-
sions that I'm living. I watched leaves land and
curl against each other. When I reached the center
of the bridge, I heard laughter from below. I was
not used to laughter so, out of profound interest, I
ran to the edge to see. I admit I was startled by the
source. There was a group, a number of persons,
clad in river colors. They had bags and weapons;*

70

they looked and called to me. Did I know them?
When I reached them, they spoke in grave tones of
a difficult yet calculated mission. There were cer-
tain things they thought I could do. The leader, a
woman, held open a suitcase inside of which lay
apparent plans. From beneath the pile of papers,
she withdrew a contraption that resembled a cir-
cuit board. She held it out to me and spoke in words
that were just barely foreign. The others of her group
had left us and were performing gymnastics near
the wall of the bridge. She wanted me to take the
mechanism from her and put it in the crevice of
the wall. I had left the house to take a walk that
day—did I say that already? Yes, perhaps they had
mistaken me. I admit that I fell in with them. The
leader placed the switch in my hand and added
more of her alien tongue. Though I conceded, slip-
ping the switch into the crevice, nothing happened
to the bridge. In fact, I took that same walk across
the bridge over the next eight days, having forgot-
ten about that experience. The day the bridge blew,
I was east of the city.

—I think I went on speaking for hours, talking
beyond the effects of the drugs, as though wel-
comed by the presence of someone

listening. Though as I say that I realize that it too may be a consequence of the drugs. I don't know all of what I told, but for a while, it felt good. Now, the uncertainty and resentment return. I wonder why I should say anything more, especially if it's true that I'm dreaming. —I am struck by the ingenuity of this idea. If I were to say aloud something like, "I'm done speaking," there would have to be a response: in answering me, my captors would have to divulge the right reality. If they talk then I know that I'm not dreaming, that I'm locked up somewhere on drugs. No, if they talk . . . Wait! I lost the relation again. Every time I feel certain that I have devised a way of procuring from my captors, or conversely from my imagination, which world I'm in, the path that I took to get there fails to maintain its shape. I reach for it and see it multiply itself by two, and as soon as I see that, it grows or lessens in dimension. The idea that I thought would save me dissipates mercilessly.

—Some talking has awakened me; there is absolute darkness in this place and no smell. I can't even sense the presence of the inanimate—a table or chair would orient me—and I believe

I'm utterly alone, so prior to existence that dust has had no time to form. However, I'm certain of that voice speaking. It repeats the same passage, though varies the tone for effect. I'm unaware of the identity and whereabouts of the supposed receiver of these words. Though I hear the words, they are not directed at me. I would have no idea how to answer such questions.

A hand slams against a surface, a light comes on, my insides respond as though set to a timer, and I begin talking. Time passes, then I stop talking. The man in front of me, who was not there a moment ago, nods his head, an encouragement to go on. Unfortunately, I have lost the inclination. I'm exhausted and there is a smudge blocking my peripheral vision. I want to ask my interlocutor what it is. But if he says nothing, I will be disappointed. I ask. He says nothing. I'm disappointed. More so, I want to pull out my hair now that I've become aware of the smudge, which is practically on top of me, in the way of bugs. I grab for my hair, but—as if I were deeply dreaming—I'm unable to isolate the specificity of my hands from the general density I presume to be my body.

A crash startles me. I turn my head. That other has fallen, still in his chair, to the floor, surrounded by the captors. They use the uniformity of their dress to intimidate him. Or am I the one intimidated by the sight of them, huddled in tan and hunched over, dropping globs of spit onto his face? He looks up, past these men, and stares without arrest at the ceiling. At first, I am perplexed by his easy fixation. Then I remember the suspended loaves of bread. I begin yelling, but am forced to stop when one of the pants begins to kick me. I'm on my back, with only my eyes free to move. And spit stings them. The bread looks delectable. Every impulse in my body tells me I want it. I scream, and then am kicked until I stop screaming, which coincides with my coming to at this table.

RADICALS PLAN

1

Monique, with the map of downtown spread out so that the group can see, is saying:

Alonso, you will be in charge of bringing the convoy up—

and wants to indicate Third Street when something tells her not to.

Up—

she is saying when she abruptly drops off.

I can't,

she thinks,

to tell them that the line on this map representing Third Street has just vanished will cause them to lose faith in me. And this is our most overt action! It will fail if encumbered by disbelief. I have to get us back on track.

However, before Monique has the chance to perform the series of postures that, when completed, should restore her proficiency, Stefani begins speaking to the group:

What Monique is trying to get across here is . . . well . . . we've got to get up early and . . . anyway . . . Alonso will have the . . . stuff and we'll be waiting outside the place for him and the sun to come up, so nobody can linger on this one. We've got to infract and dislocate, right, baby?

The group turns to M. for confirmation.

Under the blaring rays of the sun, the core members of the CPL are gathered. It's time to push forth a plan to stop the swarm of corporate America. As the slogan goes, "It takes one captain." Lomarlo is weak with hunger, leaning a bit on S. He considers the map and wonders how they will get the convoy to the site on time, but when he opens his mouth, there is only a yawn, and before he can elaborate, Freddie takes his place. He says to himself:

I'll finish up when Freddie's done, but I wonder what I can say? The group seems tired this morning. I know I'm tired. I need to tell someone that when I look at that map I see nothing but blank space. The "city grid" Monique keeps referring to is a cloud as far as I can discern. I've been there, though. I know what it's like. The place is a complete circuitry of avenues. But now, gazing at it in abstract, it may as well be a golf course. And Monique just placed our men in the pond! What should I say? The others have stepped closer, but nobody's twitching, no one is squeezing his eyes closed, or shaking his head—

Lomarlo, what's wrong with you,

Stefani asks, having noticed a shudder move through him.

He wants to say that he is very tired, that he was awake all night researching ways to battle anxiety, but he doesn't want to seem ill-fitted for the job.

I'm cold,

he confesses.

When Stefani turns back to Monique quickly as though something has caught her eye, she does not indicate, either way, her belief in him. But to herself:

Okay, what's going on here? Monique's standing there like concrete . . . Lomarlo's trembling like an idiot . . . Freddie won't stop interrupting and Alonso is reticent.

She turns her head from one to the other, but subtly so that no one notices.

Monique, still intent on the map, has to clench her jaws to keep her composure. The group has grown silent behind her. She is afraid to turn around.

I have to stay focused,

she thinks.

Then it occurs to her:

Hey, I can change the plan!

She says aloud:

*No, let's move the convoy up Edison Avenue . . .
yes, this puts us closer to the water. That way, if
anything goes wrong we can hide on the relief boats.*

From behind, there is a murmur of consent: it
seems possible to turn around. She does, and
the look on their faces fortifies. She recites the
remainder of the plan—almost to the point of
singing, but stops just short. She kind of hums.

* * *

The group dispersed only to reconvene at the
same café the next day. This time they are sitting around a table and the map is spread out in
front of them. Being out of the sun takes pressure off those most vulnerable to it, namely
Lomarlo and Monique. Both regard the sun with
suspicion. Inside, the softer natural light makes
them all happy. They are laughing and clapping
their hands. It seems that the plan makes sense.
Monique opens a briefcase on the table top and
removes a box of Lego-like toys:

*I've brought these to represent our men. Please keep
in mind that the colors pertain to our scripted
movements. Blue moves on the right side of the
street, yellow along the left.*

She then turns to the map and uses her index
finger to indicate the corner where Lomarlo
should wait with the truck.

He nods confidently, but inside himself, despairs:

*She's waiting for me to look at that map. I can't do
it. And why is it all so frenzied?*

He's worried; he can't hear everything she's saying. Someone is humming and Stefani has her hand on his leg. She's trying to calm him, but the gesture only intensifies his stress. He begins to panic that he has said something to the group without having first approved its release:

My lips are wet as though I've just been speaking. But there is nothing recognizable in my head.

Freddie is sitting on the other side of Lomarlo, thinking:

There is nothing I can say that won't sound like defection to Monique, but something is not right about that map. Or not right about the way she relies on it. She hovers above the map with her arms spread out and moving, as if at any moment she'll need to grab the corners and tuck the thing away . . .

Sometimes Freddie gets pulled inside his mind, though he considers himself an extrovert, and while there, finds himself amid startling opinions. He is embarrassed by his doubt. He tries to project M.'s words onto the screen in his mind and isolate those that disturb him.

Every few phrases,

he thinks,

*she utters a word that is completely out of the con-
text of all else she's saying. The word takes me some-
place unexpected, a place I recognize. Perhaps, the
scene of an earlier action. But when I'm in this
place—it must be an accident—I feel somehow left
behind. It lasts less than a second, though. I walk
around a room, a warehouse, a vacant street. I stare
at graffiti, which I recognize as belonging to our
group. I try to recall the coded message. I have
enough time to feel nostalgic or to remember the
pain of failure—we were not always successful—
before I return to the present. And I know in the
most reliable part of my mind that I've been gone
no more than a second. Monique says something
like "thus" or "through" and I am caught up . . .*

So,

she's saying,

*Edison is not a street that cops associate with dis-
sent. It is too narrow and too unbroken by alleys*

86

and sub-avenues for an act so risky as infiltration.
That's why I think this plan ingenious!

Stefani loves when M. becomes excited. Right
now she wants to grab her and fall down in that
patch of sun she's been eyeing across the street
and roll around until they're exhausted, but for
Monique that would be unleaderlike. When in
this predicament, where she can't express her
affection for Monique, S. settles for a speech:

Monique, this plan scintillates. It calls to mind the
brilliance of the Ascott mission, except it is worlds
more charged, sure to make known our power to
push back against tyranny, to do it in the dark of
the night, among comrades, with rage, and totally
organized. The capitalists will crumble in our
storm. Yes, we are the new militant beasts!

This last declaration calls each member's wandering mind to attention. While the pitch of the
utterance can be fastly characterized as Stefani's
pitch, its authenticity is entirely suspect for most
of the group. Alonso recognizes her, but the rest
do not. Stefani, at once, registers the discomfort
and obvious fluster of concern that infects them.

However, her struggle to recall the precise words of her speech, to then correct them, yields no reward.

Oh no,

she bemoans,

did I say "monsfriki" again?

There is a language that distinguishes this group from the other activists in the city, a language they fall into when they are together, that they do not know on their own. At times, one or two of them say words that the other three, or just one, does not know, and it causes a breach between them. The words usually are the diaphanous ones.

If I said "monsfriki" they are feeling alienated. How could I let that slip?

S. looks from one group member to the other:

Alonso looks all right, but Lomarlo appears to be choking. These are my friends, though; they know

me. If I said "monsfriki" it could have been only
with the best intentions—

Pa se cahini chini!

Monique shouts, and the barrage begins. The
friends are unusually agitated. The plans, still
spread out on the table, are accumulating stains
of water and grease, while everyone says what
they think they know about "monsfriki." Stefani
has no choice but to wait. She wants to defend
herself, her clumsy choice of words, but they
won't let her in. Her eyes begin to water, then
wander away from their faces to less animated
objects. They rest on the map:

What's that?

A white cloud spreading across the surface of
the map catches her eye.

Wait! Isn't that Edison?

Stefani puts her finger on the spot of the vanished street and turns to alert the group. But, as
she opens her mouth, a sudden doubt overrides:

What's going to happen if I tell them what I've seen? And what if I go to speak and can't say it right?

She moves her finger away, but keeps her eyes fixed on the spot. Where a second ago there was a white cloud-like mass, now there are thirty or so microscopic lines making a grid of the Edison–Chamber intersection. The grid reminds her of a virus and makes her skin itch; it's so little, so proliferating. When Stefani begins to scratch furiously at the side of her head—her hand buried so deeply in the locks of her hair that she almost discovers the secret chamber— all banter ceases. Lomarlo takes out his pen and writes her a quick note, which reads:

I've seen the map mutate too. Let's meet later.

Everybody at the table got a good view of L. scripting that note. In fact, the urgency of it calmed them. They assumed he had written something they would all support. In Monique's mind, the note read:

Hey, Stefani, pull yourself together for your woman and the cause.

Freddie, more imaginative, immediately thought:

Isa ma unitica. The world is round.

Alonso refused to project his thoughts.

Each feeling himself so separate from the others began to grow tired, to grow heavy with that unassailable exhaustion —fear. The meeting was called a day.

2

This city swelters in September, and all, from every aspect of life, pour out into the street. News gets around on sweaty lips; the police guard the goods in full force. Detritus in the streets, my lids so heavy; I see by instinct. I'm lying in the park, hidden in the uncut grass, imagining a city grid. A map of summer colors and geometry. A circumference that's doing something, the inner life of a line. All day I pretend I understand. I walk when others walk; I dance when they dance. This map, I've been so close to without touching, at which I've barely glanced—

When the grass is this high, the neighbors want it cut. But the park keepers can't stand the loss of beauty. They hold out as long as they can, inventing reasons for preservation. This time, there is an endangered beetle to protect. I'm not invested in the beetle . . . I have not seen him though I've been here all day . . . but I'm closer to believing this story than last year's. Since noon, there has been a group of whites marching along the edge of the park, cheering for the grass to be cut. They worry that we are doing drugs in the weeds—that the colored people are. Because I'm lying in the grass, representing that scenario, the noise is loudest around me. They chant *Save our park!* and *We can't see the trees!* in unison. These are the people I imagine filling the offices of downtown, who drive me toward that map. The map . . . it has become everything to us: we cannot control it but neither of us wants to say this. Even I, who cannot decipher the map, never having grasped the logic of geometry, know there is something unnerving about it.

We stole the map from the Office of Transportation and now I think the Feds set us up. If I'm wrong, then all this mutating indicates we've moved into an alternate reality, one whose principles of space and intention differ drastically from that which all our lives we've grown used to. But . . . I don't know. Reality is not static—its properties are in constant flux, so perhaps we are as much in the world as we can ever be, and that's the problem.

Whatever the case, the existence of an auxiliary presence cannot be denied. But how easy it is to become paranoid when you are an activist! Paranoia cousins you in every encounter, every look given. Your mail comes and you must receive it with an extraordinary nonchalance, almost tossing it back at the carrier from lack of concern. Strangers ask you for the time and you are compelled to express your patriotism. That is, when you are the kind of activist we are: when you steal important documents and unleash computer viruses, when you try to overthrow the mainstream. Someone is always looking for you.

I've just had to slap my arm . . . a thing was crawling up it. I hope the glob isn't the beetle. Now I'm rubbing my legs, now my lower back. A sweating body languishing in high grass begins to itch from the friction, from the heat and the marchers' now-tired chants. The words hover, foreign to the mouths that emit them. Without meaning. Projected thanks to the physics of yelling, but that's all.

Without meaning, I'm wearying of the grass and the burn of not-scratching. *Get up now,*

I'm saying. *Go on. The group is waiting for you.*
If some faction is reading my mind, please know
I'm utterly dedicated to this group. I would do
anything for them. So don't mistake my hiding
in the grass. I want to destroy that map. Plain
and simple. If we use it, I'm sure it will cause
our demise. Nothing can dissuade me from this
certainty.

the map = drama, stress, danger, uncertain + maybe death

* * *

An indiscernible time later, Alonso and his friend
Barry are lying in the high grass of the park.
Relaxed, not as though hiding. Small dogs chase
each other around the men's heads and over their
chests. The owners are pacing the sidewalks.

It's not an extraordinary day,

Alonso begins by saying.

No, not a secret at all,

Barry replies.

Your group blew up the J. Gifford Bridge.

*There is no way we could have blown up that
bridge. And Barry, the media wants to sedate you.
Everybody. The J. Gifford Bridge is one of many
distortions. I would argue that it's still there. But
all of that aside, can you help?*

Yeah . . . just tell me what to do.

First, I want you to get a look at that map. See if it mutates. If it does, understand why, then report back to me. After that, I will devise a plan to destroy it.

Well, there's no graph I can't delineate . . . but your group is intense. What if they catch me?

No, they trust you . . .

A dog pushes its way between them. The interruption allows Barry some moments to reflect.

The birds fly high over this park,

he thinks to himself against a small buzzing in his ears.

The birds fly high over the park,

he thinks again.

Plus, those are seagulls.

Why not work this out openly with the group?

Barry returns.

*It's delicate with us, particularly this action . . .
something so poignant about it that the idea of
there being a flaw is unbearable. We would have
to divest ourselves of our concerns simultaneously
to withstand the awkwardness, but that is nearly
impossible to plan. And I've already told you too
much.*

Why? You said they trust me.

*In turning to you—it's like I'm reaching my arm
out of a whirlwind. The magnitude of that . . .*

*Your arm out of a whirlwind? See that's why I could
never join one of your groups. Your whole life becomes its survival. I would hate to need any thing
so much.*

Yeah . . . but on the other hand, you utterly belong.
[The endangered beetle again] *Every space in your
mind is utilized . . . just about every space.* [He
doesn't want to swipe it] *You occupy a constant
state of detection . . . how to get to the truth . . .
how to intercept your enemies' plans.* [He blows

on it] *For example, the map. Well, you know I can't read it. I'm a blind man as far as it's concerned. I only know something is wrong because of the energy of my crew: every time the map is out, I have a heightened sense of them. They become quiet and lost in themselves. I can't hear what they're thinking of course, but I know they're struggling. Especially Lomarlo, who's always pressed to keep his head up.* [That beetle appears stuck to his arm. He's wondering if it's been planted there. He looks at Barry . . . Barry's thinking. Seems innocent. And the bug, not causing the expected itch . . . it seems innocent too. Alonso sits up and closes his eyes to the paranoia. There is a familiar quiet in his mind; however, he is incapable of speech. All he can think is, *Barry, you know what I mean.* Lying down again, he lifts the beetle from his arm, cups it in his hand, and rolls away from Barry. He puts the cupped hand under his ear. Allows the beetle to enter him. The tickling sensation of bug legs in the ear canal quickly becomes a cause for hilarity. Alonso laughs, gripping his sides, and reaches toward Barry for protection.]

3

The group assembles at a new location the following Sunday. We do not know the consequence of Alonso's encounter with Barry. We have been under the freeway with Lomarlo and Stefani. They have had their clandestine meeting. It went like this:

Why is the map mutating?

I don't know.

Then a half hour of silence.

But now, the group has reconvened and each member's relief is apparent. They are in the park across the street from the café. Some boys are playing a game of soccer around the blanket where they're sitting. It's as though they are picnicking in the middle of a field. The map, still folded, is near Monique. What they are doing is chitchatting, which is natural for them. But it should not last much longer.

Istah mahini . . . pá cá se?

Stefani interrupts in her earnest style of speech. Her friends are slow to give their attention, though each knows she's trying to save them: they sense she wants to discuss the mutations. Finally all eyes are on her; she points to the map. She prepares her mind to deliver something powerful, but as she opens her mouth a soccer player falls on top of her. Two fall on Monique and one stumbles over Alonso. Lomarlo and Freddie begin to yell, *This is absurd,* to the bodies thrashing on the ground, and the ball bounces away.

maybe an indicator that the plan won't work

maybe fate is at play

What a mess the soccer players have made. Their teammates are shouting at them: *Where is the ball?* The teammates think someone is hiding the ball or that it's flattened beneath the mess of bodies. What had been their picnic blanket is now snaked around knees and legs. Bread and cheese is on faces and the liquids are soaking the ground. Everyone is enraged. The teammates on the sideline are furious at their clumsy crew, yelling, *shit, shit,* to get their attention. This could go on for hours. Stefani, with her head between an elbow and a leg, remembers the map. *Who's got the m-a-p,* she spells out in a quiet voice, hoping only her friends will hear. Alonso says he's got it. Meanwhile, one of the players spots the ball bound for the other side of the street and the whole team takes off after it. The CPL is left in the wake of their hurry, bouncing around like boats.

TOUR

"Leaders declare today's rally outrageous" is the headline of the article I'm poised to write. My mind raided by the voices of this afternoon. The public . . . pulse of the public. I was among throngs at the nation's capital . . . citizens in uproar over the President's announcement. In the heart of something—what was it?—that's what I'm trying to uncover. At the time of the protest, the President had not actually revealed his news—there was an "internal delay"—but it seemed both sides understood what his stance would be. The right was already celebrating and the left was up-in-arms. Their not-knowing seemed to energize them more than knowing ever could. That will be one of my arguments.

So, in the field, I began where any good reporter would—with my elders. A nice gray-haired couple standing just inside the gates:

Excuse me. I'm from the paper. I see you're wearing matching Stars and Stripes sweat suits . . .

That's because we're Americans!

And what is your stance today?

America for Americans!

Don't you mean the reverse?

That's right! Americans!

Their devotion was extraordinary. However, I could not get them to comment further. They stood with their hands clasped, beaming with some inaccessible wisdom, turning their heads to imbibe all the hustle about them. I shouted, *We're Americans,* to see if I could get them to carry on. Their repudiation was unbearable, in that it was the most high-spirited display of disaffection I'd ever seen. I slunk away.

Strategically, I walked around the edge of the dense crowd, looking for dangling protesters—those having trouble getting swept in. I knew how they were feeling. What is it about momentum that there is always an inside and an out? And why is it that the people who are often out are the loneliest people? Whatever the nature of alienation, I know it makes one eager to talk.

I have not reached that level of reporting that makes for precise rendering. That skill comes after years, perhaps decades, of devoted and informed observation. Nevertheless, I recorded this afternoon's interviews. All I have to do is play and replay this tape, and in the end, I'll have a story. But how I wish I had visuals to accompany these words, not photographs but moving pictures. Something to capture the complete circuitry of the person. However, my superiors had not thus provided for me.

What I wanted was to get to the bottom of things—as in any archeological work—to suss out the source. The question, which even at this moment I'm turning over in my mind, is the nature of protest. What is it—beyond the issues? What makes one go outside and scream?

Though not all were screaming today. For example, an older man I found eyeing the crowd:

Yes, sir. From here I watch each group thunder past, but I'm too entrapped by their fervor to make my own decisions. I have scores of opinions though. Unfortunately, they oscillate.

Between what and what?

Well, when I'm able to think about it, it's some-thing like causality and prior karmic imprints. What I mean is . . . just take a look at this world: one moment, one act, splinters into an infinite number of isolated and unequal events, and yet that moment is only one of an infinite number of events having already been stimulated. So how then can you act, or rather, identify your act out of the proliferation of others? If I start screaming "Stop the war" or "Start the war" . . . you know and then I just get confused.

So what are you doing here?

The old man heard sarcasm in that question. Not true. I felt we shared something; I wanted to make him the center of this piece. To have a living encapsulation of my ideas. He walked away from me. But with trained obstinacy, as I watched him shuffle off, I devised a plan to commandeer him. I reckoned it would help if I appeared weaker than he, so as he got about fifteen feet away, I let out a scream and pretended to faint. As I collapsed, though, some kid with glitter covering his red face began to swirl violently around me.

*I've got it in my mind to pull the cork on all these
motherfuckers!*

What's that you're saying?

*I'm talking about the goddamned sacrilegious left.
We are at war, hippies! Every single one of them . . .*

I didn't stay with him long—he frightened me—
but I did lose track of the old man. Not to
worry—my story was taking shape right before
me. I knew what I needed. More old men. I
walked around, I imagine, with a fire in my eyes,
and perhaps it's this that drew the attention of
the security guards.

You have to let me see your press pass.
You need the yellow pass.
You need the square pass with the yellow stripes.
This is a catering license.
This is not a pass.

I believe they were afraid of my ability to record.
I tried to explain the First Amendment . . . God,
how the wind blew. Hear it now as I play back
the tape. My arguments were futile. They said,

111

Shut up and confine your research to the populated areas. This was obviously an infringement. But what could I do? I was alone; I didn't even have a cameraman. It is true that the approved areas had a wealth of old men; however, dejection is infectious. It starts in your ears and soon paralyzes your entire body. I stood there throwing my right leg out so that the other one would move. And was intercepted by this gentleman:

Please understand how free you are in America.

Excuse me?

You are a reporter?

Yes.

Please know that you are in a free country?

I am a neutral observer.

You don't like this country.

Yes, I live here.

Then, yes, you are very free.

I don't know. What was happening to my story?
I hadn't come across many activists. At least, not
any that made sense. I remember earlier some
guy shouting that people are enraged—certainly
true—but miserably inarticulate, also. Even me.

I am M. from the midnight crew.

Of what?

M. from the cleanup crew.

Oh.

I am you are.

Sorry?

*He says he's U. R. from the crew, too. We're just
waiting to clean up.*

I spun around—

Every single one of them motherfuckers . . .

I was walking in circles. Those birds . . . the wind.

Everybody needs to stop talking about America.

Are you here for the protest?

That is, we are all here. That is, we are here, thus America.

So what you want is . . .

No. You're wrong. It's America this, America that . . . I've had it.

What should we do?

In a sense, we should be pulling hairs from our hearts. Looking at those hairs, and investigating their origins.

So you don't believe there is war?

What we have here is a line to cross, both of us right now, giving up everything we think is right.

For what?

For nothing.

And my own fallout:

Those birds . . . I remember the days when there were pros and cons, when there was a clear positive and an equally strong and clear negative. When one side would hail signs saying "right" and another side would scream or chant "wrong." They'd do this for a few hours, then everybody would go home. The crews would come out and recycle all the mess. It would be done. This new phase we've entered, where truth is in a perpetual state of contrast. People now love to second-guess themselves, consider every possible angle. Journalism . . . it's the great sweep. Those birds . . . in the past, did they congregate among us? Of course, I can recall having seen one or two in the late sixties, soaring above. But this! And these ribbons of bats.

. . . Nothing to the tape after that, just some buzz, some hurrays. A few drunkards. *I'm a reporter,* I kept telling them to see how they would respond. But my occupation was of no consequence. I wonder what happened to that old instinct: a stick in my face makes me want to speak. Now speech is hardly noteworthy. It's only what one has thought.

"We have a dangerous fugitive on our hands,"
Daniel Sharpe of the Brendan Seize Unit (BSU)
declares with obvious emotion. "If we do not
catch her, the ensuing damage will be irrepa-
rable." Troops have gathered downtown around
"The Square," a meeting hall for two-thirds of
the city's activist groups, in a kind of dogwatch.
The men appear invincibly focused. Monique
Wally was being held at the central police sta-
tion on thirty counts of trespassing, in addition
to charges of possession of "potential destruc-
tive devices" and attempting to blow up a bridge,
when a group of radical youths stormed the
building and broke her free. No arrests have been
made, though officials say they have "tremen-
dous" leads. It is unclear whether this event is
related to the sudden increase of graffiti around
the city, most often conferring the word, "No."

NEVER AGAiN
ANYWHERE

You say:

—Monique, if . . . well, will you?

She says:

—Yes.

And then you are miserably awake.

That body clings to your morning, to the shade as you pull it, to the plant you move to get to the shade, to the sheets you return to. You wrap your arms around . . . cradle the head, turn the body over, slide onto it. I've gone. You're away. They're lying in the drying sheets, sleeping then fucking. She rolls away for coffee. You wake to pull the shade. I say, my plant's expecting light. They're in bed. The night is over.

Outside. Never there. She sits on the bed, almost pouting. Waiting for the phone. Please stop ringing. Never outside again. It is easy to reach and take the nipple in your mouth, easy to travel slowly between the legs. Someone once made a joke about the easiest way to get a woman to smell. I remind you. You reach for my head. They: one standing, the other sitting on the edge of the bed. Then both kneeling. Days pass.

Outside becomes a terrible dream, a virus erupt-ing, the mind full of doubt. So instead. Every-one uses the body for escape. A few with com-plete sincerity. I want you to show me. She's afraid. I'm afraid. I thought so.

Please stop the phone ringing. Stefani, it's Lomarlo . . . we've got to go outside. No, the last time we left. Once, they left. Never again. Tell me, why would I leave. Because it's Lomarlo.

Around two o'clock the sun moves to this win-dow. It languishes here. And I wait, lying against your pillow. What did I say that night . . . to get you to . . . ? All you said was, come outside. And you went.

S. stays. M. goes. S. is behind. M. promises to return. It's just for a time, for some training. Before, in hiding, they couldn't go outside, then they went and found things normal. Because things were normal, Monique left. S. didn't want to go. Never again. But it's my responsibility. You don't believe her.

It's never again because of danger. But danger will find you here, too. I'll just wait for her. They: but we need you. Dissidence does not go away because your lover . . . The phone rings. She says, but I'm alone. He calls. Please stop. And there is a message.

Stefani, we're coming over to get you and take you downtown to the water, and there you'll have to make a choice. He says it simply. We miss you. And ends with this: the city removed the concrete that suppressed the water and now we have a river. Then hung up. They've spent the morning staring at the shade covering the window saying, you should pull it up. For several days now they've been inside. They: she has the impression of the hand still inside her. The force of which brings on sleep. It is after then that they wake and stare at the window. The phone is no longer ringing because the person calling is coming over. She writes this on a sheet of paper and places it on the refrigerator door. I used to know what this means.

You said, never again anywhere, and then five minutes later left with us. I wanted to stay near you. I was afraid. You were afraid. What did you say to get me to go? I said. But this time she swears never to leave. What happened to Monique? She doesn't know. Looking at those words: ringing because the person calling is coming over. And repeating them again and again in her mind. Calling is coming over. The phone is no longer ringing. You quickly survey the room. Everything is clean. M. would say, you're all right, and touch your face. Then she would go back to sleep.

It's the worst kind of cycle, the one accessible only in dreams. The one you can see but not name or name but not see. The indefatigable past consuming all texture of the present. The milk that is no longer milk. You are trying to drink. The food you crave that is no longer in the cupboards. The hands that pulled the shade and touched the plant. But admit she made you promise. And confess that you agreed. Then explain how we have lost you. Is talking to me. Lomarlo, Freddie, Alonso are talking to me.

The cycle breaks momentarily when suddenly you are surrounded by your friends. Now there is a map and pamphlets on your kitchen table. The word "plans" seeming to hover. Their voices. Strange in tone, too deep and hollow. She thinks. They're not suffering. You observe Lomarlo; he talks more than he used to. Which was just some weeks ago. Pick up the map, someone says. I'm not touching. Why have you given up? It's wrong. His is most hollow. The men refuse to leave. Almost funny. After hours of silence, they say, confess that you made a promise.

A day passes. She leaves her room because there is an unfamiliar smell. The kitchen is empty; those elusive words still on the refrigerator door. Music, perhaps, coming from the front room. The audacity of invasion clouds whatever relief you feel in not being alone. The smiles they turn on you, the food you are fed. Every event pretends it is the accumulation of isolated occurrences. Then she sits down because she remembers. Look at the map, he says. They are thinking, we'll bring her back.

The afternoon Monique left she swore she would return. She did not have to swear, I told her, I had not thought otherwise. Then there was a raid. There were arrests. Also, some fleeing. Twenty-one days after M. left, she was due to return. On the twenty-sixth day, I was no longer mobile. On the thirtieth day, the forty-first. There were a few more days before she stopped counting. Now a question pervades the house. She doesn't know.

Now they have dressed her in black and are pushing her out the door. Herd me down the street. The wet street and cold now that it is night. Now that she is where she vowed to never be. Now on a bus, now down stairs, faces leaning. Freddie whispers codes and doors open. She accepts the old days. They rest me against a wooden stand, then take seats in front of me. From the back of the room a chant begins, which, once it arrives to the front, sounds like "speak, speak." I have nothing to say.

One body, inhaling at the same time to the same capacity. Then exhaling. I'm trying to say we shouldn't time our breathing. We shouldn't time our breathing, she manages to say.

The room erupts in applause.

WHiTE CiTY

The group goes anyway, though everything has changed; other organizations show too. Some still in their bedclothes, which they must have been wearing when they heard the news. We have to keep moving—that's what the media says. But our plan to protest globalization in a coherent circle around the towers is ineffectual without the towers, which were destroyed earlier today. So we're all skipping to part II of the plan: post-op assessment. The CPL enters the meeting hall, having said little to each other on the walk there. Everything worth uttering is immediately repealed by the white almost-plaster on our clothes. We enter and disperse quickly—each of us going off to a corner of her own. We sit and turn our white away from the other without prompting. All reasons are plain; there are no towers to swarm and this is because we hadn't thought to protect them.

A man utters something slowly as though having to translate the sentiment from a complex language. No one seems to understand. So he repeats the sentiment as if in its original language. It is difficult to know what to do with such information. There are fifty-five chairs in this room; I count and recount them until it is my turn to speak.

Lifting my body from the chair, stepping through our dust across the floor to the podium. Against the noise of the projector, I pronounce these spontaneously generated words. The act is the greatest physical achievement of my life. And the speech I give is no good.

I say, *All . . . everything . . . today . . . nothing is to have and nothing is to have . . .* I cannot proceed because I do not know what pronouns to use. I do not want to speak rhetorically and yet I am standing at a podium. If I say "he" or "she" it will seem that I am deflecting responsibility onto others, absolving myself. I go on for fifteen minutes in the ellipses described above, hoping in the end to have made sense. But I hear little response from the fog.

The place in my speech that pulls them out of their stupor is where I talk uninhibitedly about the impact of our missions on inadvertents. Apparently, we all harbor guilt around those we've inconvenienced, and my words touch on that. I say, *Were . . . had any people who . . . made wait or walk long distances . . . today . . . had to find them and apologize . . . too much to explain . . . complaint with American capitalist structures.* I want to say, "We find that we can't agree," but that would be committing to two personal pronouns. Who could face that?

Looking over the room, through the white dust, elongated light as always in this place on this type of day, I watch a fly turning. Someone clears her throat: I must have ceased speaking. Two women I do not recognize begin to move toward me. I think I am being usurped. Not because I have done anything wrong: the groups just can't stand the silence. Speech is a necessity and I am speaking, but the sounds I emit are cobbled with dirt. My mouth is open, my tongue moves. I say *ur* and *were* and pant in between. It is not enough.

Sitting in my chair again, I look over to Monique and want to be with her. She's on the other side of the room. There are chairs around her and thick white particles floating toward the window;

I imagine others shrouded behind the cloud. There is a new person at the podium whose body is incomprehensible. I want Monique with twice the ferocity with which I wanted her last night, desperate to throw my arms around something warm and breathing.

I want to sit near you . . .

I try to send over from my mind.

A series of coughs interrupt my posturing. They are coming from me and from the shadows off to my right. I forget that we are having difficulty breathing, that we feel as though we have inhaled bits of glass. I attempt to refocus my attention by putting the index and middle fingers of both hands to my temples. Everybody is coughing, even the speaker. Someone shouts, *Open the windows or close them.* We turn around to see which is the case. Moments later they are closed; a fan, high above, is going.

The speaker continues. A man's voice. He speaks more coherently than I, but utterly without emotion. I'm sure everyone wishes to blend my fever with his didactics. He is all right. We are less afraid with him there.

After a few minutes more of his speech, I remember my previous desire to be near Monique. I turn to her. She is there, watching me, with her hand covering the face of her watch. I can see two socialists sitting on either side of her, talking to each other across her back. She does not appear to know they are there. The projector continues its clack. I begin to feel weak trying to hold her gaze; it is deciphering. She is reading me, undressing me, something. So depressed she is—I can see it weighing on her face—such a concerted effort to keep me when I am going nowhere.

I'm still here . . .

I try to send over from my mind.

I guess my thoughts can't penetrate the cloud that I forgot enveloped me. And I'm struggling to maintain my form against the pressure of the projector and the monotonous speaker. We are all wrapping our arms around our heads, trying to quiet the thoughts inside or trying to seclude the thoughts from the terror of outside. Everybody, actually, is doing something different. Not all arms are wrapped around all heads. Some people are sitting upright, perfectly poised, except for some part of them that is trembling. The towers were destroyed and there is no news to otherwise disclaim this fact.

The projector is going, but no one has inserted the reel: it is white light. The post-op assessment is failing. Well . . . we didn't accomplish anything. I search the room for clues. Should I reverse everything we have just done: open the windows, turn off the fan, gather us in a circle? Should I turn off the projector, reclaim the stage? Is there an entirely different series of gestures that we haven't thought to do? Should we adjourn for the day? Wait for further action? Complete an action, then meet?

Questions and the light projecting the white lifting from our clothes. The inside-outside dynamic. Activists on the inside? The city unsung in a matter of minutes. And now these images. Population running. Hard breathing and white

dust. Felt the explosion; I did not see it. I know
I am getting somewhere; however, seeing my
comrades' faces, I also know I am running out
of time. Where is Monique, I think?

News floats up: *The President says we're at war.*
And the minute threads connecting us break.
We trash the room. We fight each other. I find
Monique, but it's too late. I want to harm her.
Everyone tries to harm everyone else—our noise
thundering around the room—until Alonso
opens a window and we pull back into ourselves.

WHiTE CiTY II

(rub is overly defined

A slow over-hunting. How the shadows look now.
How the shock of self-exposure inanimates a
room of exposed selves. When there is less light
how the white particles disappear. Rather, how
we forget that they are floating and see them
only as stained into our clothes. The voice on
the radio, how it disseminates the news. And
the fifteenth person at the podium. The clack-
ing of machine. I'm pretending that my arm does
not hurt, that you did not hurt me. This building was once a courthouse. How the walls are
still paneled in wood. How the high ceilings give
us the sense that we're succeeding. We assign
value to these objects, not to the cut on the face
that's still bleeding or the socialist crying in the
corner. And the radio continues with its news.
We are all one, it says, against an abominable
enemy. And the person turns to me. I take the
stage.

A slow over-hunting, is what I'm thinking, but
what I say is, *Comrades we have a decision to make.*
Because I'm a leader, some begin to lean toward
me. How can I say, when we are so disheart-
ened, that we have devoted too much time? Let's
give everything up and sit alone in our rooms.

141

Who said we should spend four hours there? How I would like to remember. *Comrades, this is not a time to act,* I finally say to the room. But those words, as they erupt from my mouth, obliterated by the projector noise. Shall I repeat myself? I want to end the over-hunting, if just for a night. So I emit louder, slower, *Let's sit with this.*

I've said it; I look at them; they have iron faces. They don't know what I mean. They do, but they don't like it.

How I long for quiet, for these faces to turn away from me—

Someone is saying, *Monique, we have to protest. We have to break this chain of retaliation.* Yes, that's true, I think to myself. I look up from the unuttered lines of my speech that continue "our choice must show the world we won't tolerate war." But all I feel is the over-hunting. Women move toward me. I think they want to help. *What do you need,* one asks, hand on my arm. I whisper, *I don't know.* She points to my speech, *Keep reading. I don't know how I feel anymore,* is my response. *Then sit down.*

I turn away from the podium, toward my seat. The image projected on the screen is of a man giving a speech to a stone-faced audience. And somewhere in my mind the sound of rain. Alonso approaches. Is he going to speak? We meet halfway between the first row of chairs and the waiting podium. He hands me a note, but it's too dark to read. I tell him, *I can't make out a word.* He says, *yes,* and pushes me back toward the stage. I'm in front of the crowd again; my mind is still empty.

The indecipherable note burns in my hand. The audience claps thinking that in my brief walk I've focused my mind and now will call them to act. I keep trying to find the light to read the note without showing them that I have it. I'm assuming it will anger them to know Alonso passed it on to me. The expectation tonight being: we are a whole. This note dictates what I should say. I'm shaking with its urgency. I have never wanted to know anything so much. These words that will justify our contempt and fortify our dedication, that will outline the unifying points of our struggle—after I read them, the white of my mind will fill again. But I am losing my spot on stage. Their patience is waning; the iron of their faces progressing to concrete structures, almost buildings. Buildings linked by a slow over-hunting, now quickening.

Monique, someone says.

Where is Stefani? *I'd like to ask Stefani to the stage,* I say. I want to make sure she's still here. I wait. Legs appear first, then torso, then face. I'm so small today. She's beside me at the podium; I hand over the note. I ask, *How do I sound from there?* She responds, *Nearly perfect. You just need to project more.* I say, *I'm worried about my conviction. Read me what Alonso wrote.* She opens the note. I take it away from her, *No, you read my speech, while I take a peek at the note.* We do this; it takes five minutes. I drink in A.'s words against the crowd's sudden roaring. The rank and file stamp and chant around the room because S. has come through again. My speech, which I wrote two hours ago when the meeting first began, is the anticipated hit. It's telling them what to do and they are beside themselves, relieved, while I'm still inside Alonso's note. He was right to give it to me.

From far away, Stefani says, *It's done.* And I thank her. There is familiar movement around the room; people are forming committees. My stomach sinks with the thought of that near intimacy, of shoulders almost touching that I want to lodge myself between. The idea of returning the note to Alonso comes easily. I walk over to him and whisper, *I need to give this back to you so I can push on with my plans,* using my palms to indicate the direction I wish to go. *Did it restore you,* he wonders, reaching toward me. I have to tell him no. *Not the words so much as—* he finishes the thought for me as I place the note in his hand and watch him curl his fingers around it. Our friends begin to wave us over. *Yes,* he concludes as we move toward them, adding some unspeakable words.

The role of speech... commentary of society
if we are unclear of who was speaking.

- lost of words (people expect someone to know what to say or do)

- we are not clear what we are looking at like the bridge
  - organization + gov't influence our power of observation.

- book playing a tendency of pointing out things